P9-CLC-427

Little Black, A Pony

By Walter Farley

Illustrated by James Schucker

BEGINNER BOOKS

A DIVISION OF RANDOM HOUSE

For Steve, who helped write it.

©Copyright, 1961, by Walter Farley. All rights reserved under International and Pan-American Copyright Conventions. Published in New York by Random House, Inc., and simultaneously in Toronto, Canada, by Random House of Canada, Limited. Library of Congress Catalog Card Number: 61-7789. Manufactured in the United States of America.
6 |365

When I was little I had a
pony. I called him Little
Black. He was my very, very
good friend.

The two of us went all over the farm.

We had fun. We went to see the other horses. We saw Big Red.

My, that horse could run!

Then one day I said, "Little
Black, I would like to try to
ride Big Red."

So I went to the barn.

I looked at Big Red.

Could I ride this horse?

Could I ride this big horse?

I could!

I could ride Big Red!

It was fun!

All my friends stopped to look at me.

I went by Little Black. But he would not look at me.

Soon I began to jump Big Red. This horse could do everything!

We jumped and jumped.

But when I went by Little
Black, his head was down.
He looked sad.

Then one day I took Big
Red out for a long ride.

What a day!

What a time we had!

Little Black came running
along right after us.

He could not keep up with
us. He tried but he was too
little.

He could not run as fast as
Big Red.

We went on.

A big tree was down.

It was in the way.

Big Red jumped right over
the tree.
To him it was just a hop!

It was not just a hop to
Little Black.

But he tried it.

He tried to jump over the
tree.

But Little Black could not
jump that high.

Down he went.

His leg was stuck.

It was stuck in the tree.

"Oh, Big Red," I said. "My pony wants so much to do everything you do! Look at him! His leg is stuck. He can't get up!

"We must go back! We must help him! Come on."

I took hold of the tree.

I had to pull, and pull, and pull.

It took a long time.

At last I got his leg out.

Then I talked to Little Black.

"Please don't try to do everything Big Red does. He is a big horse. You are only a little pony. You could get hurt."

I talked and talked to him. I wanted him to be happy.

But he would not look at me.

He just looked sad.

So I was sad, too.

Days went by.

Then I took Big Red out
again. Little Black came along
too.

But he did not hold his head
up.

He did not hold his tail up.

He just looked sad.

We went down to the river.
It was so hot! I sat down
under a tree. Big Red went
into the water. He went way
out. There the water went
very, very fast.

Little Black put two feet into the water.

Was he going to do just what Big Red did?

Was he going out in the fast water, too?

"Come back here, Little
Black," I said. "You could get
hurt."

I took hold of him. I pulled
him back.

"You can't go out there!
The water is too fast for you.
Don't try to do just what Big
Red does! He is a big horse!
You are just a little pony."

After that day, Little Black
was more and more sad.

He would not look up when
I went to see him. I guess he
thought he was no good at all.

He did not eat very much.

When I tried to give him
apples, he would not eat them.

This made me very sad.

Little Black was my friend.
I wanted him to be happy.

One morning it was very cold.

Just as the sun came up, I looked out.

There was Little Black.

My friend, my good little
pony, was running away.

I had to get him back!

I ran down to the barn and
jumped on Big Red. "Hurry!
Hurry!" I said. "We must go
and get my pony!"

We went out of the barn
fast.

We could see Little Black's
tracks in the snow.

On and on we ran in the snow. We went right along in the tracks of Little Black.

But I could not see him.

"Little Black," I called.

"Please come back! I love you more than any horse!"

Then we came to the river.
The river was all ice!
Big Red did not like the
look of that ice.
He stopped.

"Come on!" I said to Big Red.

"Little Black is over there in the trees! He went over the ice! You can, too! Come on! Try it!"

He did try it!

But the ice did not hold Big
Red.

Crack! Splash!

Down I went.

Down I went into the cold
water.

Big Red got back up on the bank.

I tried and tried to get there too.

But I could not.

My feet were cold.

My hands were cold.

I was cold all over.

"Help! Help!" I called.

But Big Red could not help me.

Then I saw something on
the other bank.

Something in the trees!

It was Little Black.

He saw me in the water.

"Help me, Little Black," I
called.

"Help me! You can run on
the ice! You are little! The ice
will hold you!"

Little Black looked at me.

He looked at the ice.

And then his head went up.

His tail went out.

He was not sad any more.

Here was something he
could do!

Little Black came.

He came to me over the ice.

"Come on, boy!" I called.

"You are going to make it."

Little Black got to me.

He let me take hold of his tail.

Then he pulled and pulled to get me out of the water.

Then he pulled and pulled to get me up on the ice.

Would the ice hold the two of us?

The ice did hold us.

And on over the ice we went!

Little Black pulled me back to the bank of the river.

"Good boy," I said. "You saved me!"

Now Little Black put his head up high. My, he was happy! At last he had done something Big Red could not do.

That night all my friends came to see Little Black.

We were all as happy as he.

"Little Black," I said, "there is no horse like you. You are the best of all! And I will ride only you from now on."